Eating Batteries

and other stories from the middle of the night

by
Ginger Collins & Pamela Griner

Diddy Pubs 2017

First Edition: November 2017
Printed in the United States of America

A Note to our Readers

These short stories look at the universal themes of motherhood, travel, friendship, and growing up—all with the twists and dark undertones that often accompany the subconscious.

We dedicate this collection to those who remember their dreams and those who patiently listen to the recounting of them the next day.

Table of Contents

Eating Batteries

and other stories from the middle of the night

For Amy P.

1974 – 2018

Part 1
Motherhood

"Life is pleasant. Death is peaceful.
It's the transition that's troublesome."
— *Isaac Asimov*

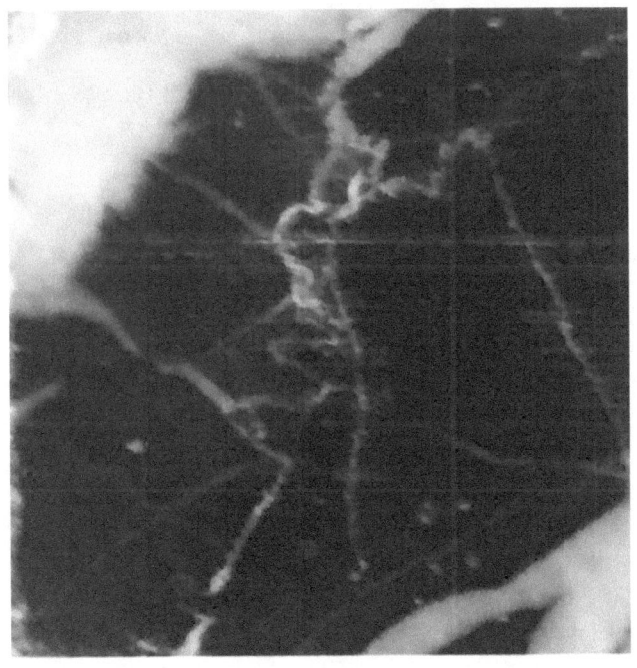

Eating Batteries

Delicious, like a chocolate truffle but without the calories. As Virginia looked around for familiar faces, she pulled one out of her pocket and popped it in her mouth.

She and her husband Eric were finally having a night out. A *real* one, with other adults and no official agenda, no dinner-and-a-movie. Virginia thought about how ubiquitous "house parties" had been in her younger days, and how, over time, they had all turned into dinner parties with essentially the same guest list and slight variations of basically the same menu. But this one felt like old times: a party at Greg's, complete with a keg and a DJ. They had all been close once, but with Greg untethered to children or family life, it had been a while since they were together.

Her toddler home in bed and her husband off to find his buddies, Virginia tried to remember what came next. A drink was typically the first step, she recalled, but drinking wasn't her poison these days. Spinning in bed with a dry mouth didn't pair well with being awakened before sunrise.

She kept a stash of triple-As with her—having a house

full of electronic trains meant batteries were always available—and she'd been snacking on them tonight. She loved how crunchy they were; she bit into the inner section and felt the sweet liquid ooze down her throat. Before her son was born she'd been quite a partier. But once she'd discovered the battery buzz, she'd never looked back. Not only was it tasty, it gave her energy, as advertised, with no hangover attached.

Virginia wandered into the backyard where there was a crowd of people dancing to Missy Elliott. She felt her groove coming back. It had been a long three years. She recognized a woman with a pink barbed-wire armband tattoo whom she knew back during her gin-and-tonic days.

"Claire?"

"Virginia! Hey! Long time!" Claire's eyes widened, surprised to see her friend. She reached out for a partial hug just as Virginia took note of a large, crusty patch of skin on Claire's forehead. It wasn't easy to divert her eyes, and Claire seemed to notice. She waved over a man standing nearby.

"Justin, have you met Virginia? I have no memory these days!"

"I don't think so," Justin said, extending his hand. "Hey there, Virginia. Justin. The husband."

Virginia grinned. "We're both married! Man, time flies."

Claire pulled Justin close and whispered something. He walked away, looking slightly perturbed, but Claire seemed unruffled.

"So you and Eric got married too?" asked Claire.

"We did, and along came baby. He's almost three now."

"Wow! We have two! I guess Greg's still holding out, huh?" Both of the women looked to the party host who was dancing with a young, sexy brunette in a tight mini-dress that barely covered her ass.

Justin returned, cracking open a can of Coke. Claire excused herself and stepped away with him to an unlit spot by a tree. Virginia's eyes followed them and watched as Justin poured a small amount of soda on Claire's head. Claire didn't resist in any way, as though she expected it. *That's strange*, Virginia thought. Justin and Claire shared a few more words before Claire dabbed her forehead with her scarf and headed back toward her.

Virginia absentmindedly reached into her pocket and tried to pop another battery in her mouth.

"Girl, you do it, too?" Claire asked with a wink.

"Do what?" Virginia tried to cover her slip up, and hid

the battery in the fleshy part of her cheek.

"Be careful. It's hard to stop." Claire seemed to know what she was talking about, and issued her advice without a judgmental tone.

Virginia was shocked. "You mean you eat them too? I never tell anybody…I just put one in my mouth one day…I don't know why, I can barely remember…the baby woke up crying and I walked in to get him from his crib in a daze and stepped on a battery…I picked it up and before I had realized what I was doing, I had already bitten it in half…I had no control!"

"Don't worry! We all do it. It's one of those things they skip over in baby class, you know, things they never tell you because you'd never believe *you* could ever be so broken or stoop so low…'that won't happen to *me*.' Has this happened to you yet?" Claire pulled her bangs apart and pointed to the spot on her forehead. The flaky white scales were mostly gone, but a few small spots remained.

Virginia squinted and strained, as if her teenage friend were asking her if her zit looked bad. "I don't really see anything."

"The acid spots. It's okay, I know you saw them. The positive ones are really hard to hide. Fortunately, the negative ones are usually hidden by my shoes."

"Negative ones? I'm not sure—"

Before Virginia could finish, Claire was taking off her slip-on sneaker, revealing crusty white toes.

"Gross, isn't it? Battery acid." Claire tipped the can and poured soda over her feet. The white spots bubbled up and then disappeared, revealing skin-colored digits once again. "It helps to always have a hat with you. And never be far from one of these." She lifted her can.

"When does…that…start?" There was no time for manners. Virginia did not want those scales on her face.

"After a couple years of using regularly. I still think it's worth it. That energy rush! But you gotta really watch it, it can get out of hand. Look around." She gestured toward a small bonfire in the corner of the yard where several people were congregated. Virginia caught sight of one woman, whose cheeks, forehead, and chin were covered in white scales.

Claire smiled at Virginia's surprised reaction. "You'll start noticing it now. I bet she forgot how long it's been since she's been doused. You need someone to have your back all the time when you get to that point. My husband hates that I do it, but he doesn't want me to end up like her, so he sticks close. Someone should tell her. Hang on, be right back."

Claire approached the woman, said something Virginia couldn't hear, and the woman immediately put her hands on her cheeks. She tipped her head back and Claire, taking a quick glance around to make sure nobody was watching, dribbled the rest of her Coke over the woman's face.

Virginia was amazed that battery eating happened on this level and that she'd never known; she'd assumed she'd been alone. She felt vindicated and wanted to tell her husband. She popped another triple-A and scanned the crowd for him. A younger woman grabbed her forearm.

"Did you just swallow that?!"

"Not yet," said Virginia, chewing as she talked, and with sudden confidence. "But I will. Why, you wanna try one?"

"No! That's terrible for you! Those are poisonous!"

"Exactly what about them is poisonous?" This young thing wasn't going to throw her.

"Battery acid, mercury, all kinds of stuff. You must know that?"

Virginia rolled her eyes. "Don't believe everything you read. How old are you?"

"Twenty-three."

"No kids yet, right?" Virginia guessed.

"God, no. Why?"

Virginia gave her a sympathetic smirk. "Oh nothing. Just tells me a lot. Enjoy your Pinot Grigio. We'll talk again in ten years." She clinked a battery against the woman's plastic stemless tumbler then turned to see Eric at her side.

He spoke low and raised his eyebrows in his new dad-is-always-right look. "How many have you had?"

"Just a few. Calm down." He always said that too many made her ornery, but she was feeling good right now.

Virginia looked around for Claire and the crusty woman. Maybe they had more tips for her. She approached the bonfire. Now that she was aware of it, she noticed there were a few other people with flakes around their temples and hairlines. Then something stopped her cold. A woman nearby was covered in what looked like icing that had dripped and hardened along the way down—off of her chin like a goatee, under her armpit, filling the small of her back—but she carried on as if nothing odd was happening. Virginia scanned the party for Claire. She needed help making sense of this. Was this woman corroding?

Seconds later, a loud boom sent everyone to the grass. Her ears still ringing, Virginia cautiously looked up. With the hip-hop awkwardly filling the silence, she realized that the icing woman had exploded. The people she had been talking to just moments prior now stood paralyzed, covered with bits of the woman's white-coated body parts.

Virginia put her hand in her jacket pocket and fiddled with her stash. The clicking noise soothed her.

Outnumbered

It was hard to get a deep breath. *Is this what they mean by thin Colorado air?* Shelly wondered. She watched her precocious five-year-old son as he navigated the frozen lake. He was surprisingly capable for his first time on ice skates. The snow sat heavily on the trees surrounding them, and the dry air was so cold her joints felt immobile, locked into position as if the ice had worked its way inside her body and settled in her elbows and knees. She shivered, bent down to feel one of her twin daughter's cheeks, and pulled the drawstring tighter around the girl's hood. They were not accustomed to these temperatures. Back home, she wore a scarf if it dipped below fifty-five.

Nyla, bundled up in a tiny and ridiculously puffy nylon suit, sat next to her on the frozen lake and happily pushed a pinecone back and forth. Some distance away with Aunt Beth, the twin's sister shouted and squealed, gleefully playing her own little games. The girls had accepted that their new walking skills didn't translate to this surface.

Her son skated over, face chapped and nose oozing, and gave his sister a shove.

"Not so rough, Max!"

He laughed and glided away then turned right around and swerved in again. He swatted his sister's head then shuffled his feet just fast enough to get away from his mother's hand, which was about to strike.

"Do not do that again! Nyla will fall and hit her head on the ice! Do you hear me?"

Max didn't give her the satisfaction of a reply.

She caught an odd sound of something whipping through the air. Alert, she swung her head around to find the source. Just then, she heard the crunching of ice and a splash. The shriek that followed yanked her attention directly to her other twin, who had fallen into a hole and was half-submerged in the frigid water.

"Oh my god! Olivia!"

The whipping sounds proliferated and cracks shot out from the hole, spreading like a web. Aunt Beth now lay sprawled on her belly reaching for the child, but between the panic and the mittens she could not get hold of her. Olivia flailed her arms and panted shallow breaths. Shelly heard Beth calling to Olivia, and then Max screaming "Mama!" She tried to run but her soles wouldn't grip the surface, and she struggled simply to stay upright. In the most horrific instant of her life, she saw Olivia slip under the ice completely.

Another series of splintering bursts suddenly expanded the crack in her direction. It was clear now that they were all in danger. Shelly looked back at Nyla, who was sitting alone a few feet behind her. Max had stopped skating in the middle of it all, crying for his mother to save him. Despite the frigid air, Shelly's head felt like it had been lit on fire. She had no idea what to do.

Her mind raced through a useless assembly of thoughts. She had to get to her drowning child; that was obvious. But what if the ice broke when she got there and she went in too? An image appeared in her mind of a person in a frozen lake drifting slowing under solid ice, not able to breathe. She cursed herself for putting everyone in this predicament: three children on the ice with only two adults and no safety precautions, no knowledge of how to handle this. She was a good parent, at least she had always thought so. How did this happen? And what would happen if she and Beth both fell in with Olivia? Who would rescue Nyla and Max? Her failures pressed on her soul from every angle.

Surrounded by screaming, she went numb. Only her head moved back and forth between the twins and her son. Olivia's splashes and yelps echoed deep in Shelly's head; her skin burned hot and wet under her heavy coat. She strained for sips of the thin air, but that too seemed to be vanishing.

Linda's House

It was a grotesque car accident on the 105 that eventually led Kelly to her dream home. Since the birth of their son, Coen, she and Rick had fantasized about having more space. Now that she was pregnant again, it was required. They packed the diaper bag, grabbed their list of open houses, and headed out.

Once they'd left the beige look-alike homes behind them, the houses became more varied, more inspired. In this neighborhood, *For Sale* signs were rare.

"There's one—ewwww," Kelly groaned.

"Ewww? What's wrong with it?"

"Don't you see the gladiolus? You know I hate that flower. It's a funeral flower. Why would anyone willingly plant it in their yard?" It was probably the hormones; her opinions were strengthened by her nausea these days.

"Are you kidding? The flowers? That's the easiest possible thing to replace."

"I'll always wonder who lived there and what other bad decisions they made."

"Ha! This mission is doomed. You are unbelievable."

He was almost right. For two hours, no matter what they saw, she found a reason to dismiss it. When Rick was just about to give up, they saw a "for sale" sign in front of a large home set back from the street on a corner lot. It had a gladiolus-free, meandering garden and a barely-visible back house that could potentially be converted into a studio or playroom.

"Not bad," Kelly said, stepping out of the car to change Coen's diaper. "Too bad there's no open house. I'll call the number."

"Hold on, it looks empty," Rick was already headed toward the house. "Let's just have a look."

Kelly opened the hatchback and laid the baby down while Rick looked into the windows of the home. His casual attitude about lingering in someone's yard bothered her. He didn't always understand social boundaries. It made her anxious.

"Nobody here!" he called. "This one is great, you gotta check it out. Floor-to-ceiling windows into the backyard! Which looks gigantic from here!" He started down the side of the house.

"Rick, stop it! Let's go!"

"Oh, c'mon," he taunted her. "We're already here, I just wanna see it."

"No." She picked Coen up and pulled his face into her chest to muffle his calls for Daddy and started loading him into the car.

Rick doubled back. "When did you become so uptight? Aren't you the same girl who streaked the library during finals?"

She glared. "We were in college, Rick. With no kids. Grow up."

"I'm just saying, Hell-Kell went all buttoned-up on me. Am I stuck with *this* you now?" He grabbed her hand.

"Fine!" She let herself be dragged around the back of the house, more to prove him wrong than because she thought it was a good idea.

"Hey, check it out…" Rick was turning the knob of the patio door.

"Do not go in there!" Kelly hissed.

"Where, in here?" he said, smiling as he stepped inside.

Against her better judgment, Kelly couldn't resist stealing a glance. It was furnished, just the basics and no clutter, as if it were staged. The kitchen dared her to not give it proper respect. Double oven. Wine refrigerator. Restaurant-grade gas range. The nearby family room was large but cozy with a gorgeous, oversized fireplace.

Rick picked up on her changed attitude. "Pretty good, right? Let's check out the upstairs."

"No. Enough."

"Okay…then I'll meet you back outside."

But she didn't leave and soon found herself carrying Coen up the stairs. By the time she got to the second floor, she was convinced they had found their new home. She pushed open the master bedroom door then quickly pulled it shut again.

"Holy shit! There's someone in there!" she mouthed, turning to Rick and thumbing over her shoulder.

"What?" Rick asked at full volume.

She scowled at him and gestured angrily with her head toward the door.

"No way," he said as he nudged past her and opened the door a few inches to see for himself.

"Hello? Honey, is that you?" a woman's voice called from the far side of the room.

They both froze, eyes locked on each other. Options raced through Kelly's mind. *Run for the door?* By the time they got the baby in the car seat, they would be caught for sure. Playing dumb was the only out.

Rick, for once, was on the same page. "We are so sorry, we thought the house was empty."

A pretty, middle-aged woman appeared at the bedroom door in a bathrobe. She didn't seem at all disturbed to see strangers in her hallway.

"Yes, we are *so* sorry," Kelly said. "We're house hunting and are having such a hard time finding something we like, and the door was open, and—"

The woman spoke as though they were expected houseguests.

"Can I get you something to drink? I'm Linda. Hello, baby!" She reached out to touch Coen. Though he had been quiet all morning, he let out a sudden wail and pulled his limbs into the carrier on Kelly's torso like a turtle. Kelly was embarrassed, but Linda was not fazed. "I love babies! Mine are all grown up. Big people now. Won't you stay? I can give you a proper tour."

"No, no, we shouldn't even be in your house. We do love it, by the way. It's the best place we've seen. By far." Kelly felt herself stammering to counteract their egregious social blunder.

"The kids are out with their dad. I need to get dinner ready. Or maybe they'll bring dinner home? I never could remember what the plan was…anyway, we have such a big family, and the more the merrier!"

Kelly and Rick shared a glance and decided the woman had issued an invitation. A door slammed.

"Mom, we're home! Let's eat!" Deep male voices came from downstairs.

"Hubby's home with the kiddos!" Linda seemed utterly elated. Kelly made a mental note to be more welcoming when Rick got home.

Linda spoke to them as she floated down the stairs. "Please don't rush off. Stay and meet everyone!"

Before they had a chance to respond, they found themselves back in the kitchen with Linda's husband and five immensely obese young-adult children. Linda's face was contorted with glee as she embraced each one, squeezing them hard and saying each of their names as she did. Kelly stared and Rick elbowed her.

"Kids, we have company! Would you look at that precious little baby? I remember when you were all babies. My oh my. Where has the time gone?"

Nobody else looked at the baby or at them; the family carried on as if the interlopers weren't even there.

"We didn't pick up dinner, Mom. There was a huge accident. That's why we're late. Should we just order pizza and wings?"

Dad's immense baritone voice boomed: "Sounds great! But you know what I'd really like to do? Watch some home movies!"

Linda nearly shrieked. "Great idea, love!" She turned to Kelly and Rick. "And you can watch them with us, so you can see how happy your family will be here!"

"Oh, is the house still for sale?" Kelly asked.

"We're practically gone already," she said. "Just having the darndest time saying goodbye!"

The family piled into the living room. They squeezed so tightly onto two sectional sofas that Kelly, seated in the middle, thought she and the baby might be squirted skyward by the spreading thighs and uncontained love handles. The projector whirred and the screen was filled with images of dad on vacation lounging in a zebra-striped Speedo, award-winning belly flops at the pool, and the children gorging themselves on Cadbury eggs and Peeps at Easter. They were an undeniably happy bunch.

Kelly whispered to Rick, "Should we go? The baby just fell asleep and I can't tell if they really want us here. They have barely acknowledged us, aside from Linda."

He nodded. They stood up to test the waters. The family was engrossed in their memories and didn't even look up, so Rick and Kelly quietly let themselves out.

As soon as they got to the sidewalk, Kelly grabbed her phone. "Oh my god! That was so weird. Weird and kind of fantastic! I want to call the realtor right now!"

"See what happens when you loosen up a little? That's the girl I married."

While Rick buckled the baby in, Kelly slid into the passenger seat and dialed Janice, who would no doubt be thrilled—her suggestions had been rejected by Kelly for many months.

"Hi Janice, it's Kelly. Guess what? We found it! We found the perfect house."

"Wow! Tell me more! What's the address?"

"213 Willow Lane. It was an unplanned stop, we just saw a sign in the yard, so we looked. It's probably out of our price range, but it's fantastic. We met the owners and they were very sweet. We can see ourselves there for a long time." She looked at Rick, and he smiled and winked back at her.

Janice hesitated. "Willow Lane…you say you met the homeowners?"

"We did! The whole, big, happy family. It was a little awkward, but we kinda loved it!" Her enthusiasm was met again with silence. Janice cleared her throat.

"Kelly, that house has been on the market for a year. I didn't put it on your list because I *never* show that house. The family who lived there was in a horrible accident. The father and kids were hit head-on by a food delivery truck. Every one of them died."

Kelly blanched. Janice continued.

"I'm surprised you didn't see it on the news. It was quite a sensational wreck. The family was so gigantic they could barely be extracted from the car. There was well over one ton of people in that vehicle. The mother was so distraught she shut herself in the house alone for weeks. Eventually a relative discovered she had hung herself in the master bedroom with her bathrobe belt."

Kelly stared at the sidewalk. *That's impossible. Those people were real.* True, the family barely seemed to notice them, but Linda had spoken directly to them, and to the baby. She recalled Coen's reaction to Linda then scrambled.

"Oh, maybe I'm wrong then, maybe they were just neighbors, I'm not really sure..."

"Kelly, I can't recommend buying a house with that kind of tragedy attached to it. It's almost impossible to block it out and live your life."

Kelly tried to regroup quickly as she listened to Janice. It was the perfect house for them. She didn't always have to go the reasonable, pragmatic route. *Hell-Kell would go for it, ghost family and all,* she thought, feeling a long-buried surge of adventure awaken. She pressed the mute button and looked at Rick. "It's ours if we want it, hon!"

"Great! When is the family moving out?"

"Janice says they should actually be out already, so, soon, I guess!"

He gave an enthusiastic thumbs-up, and Kelly unmuted the phone.

"Janice, thank you for all the information. We want to make an offer."

She looked at the house, which again seemed empty, though she swore she could see a light flickering in the family room.

Part 2
Wanderlust

"There is always somebody about to ruin your day, if not your life."
— *Charles Bukowski*

Pammy in a Backpack

Not long ago, Marylou saw an episode of *South Park* in which Randy Newman was banished to the bottom of the ocean. As pleased as she was to see that rotten man publicly ridiculed, she also felt her stomach clench into a painful knot. She had never been able to forgive him for writing "Short People." Her older and taller sister had antagonized her with that song when they were young. *"They got grubby little fingers and dirty little minds, they're gonna get you every time,"* she'd sing while she chased Marylou around the house until she had her cornered, pinning her down while she sang inches from her face.

Marylou grew up believing that she was unnaturally small and less worthy than her sister and all the people around her who were taller. Slow but continual growth through high school and college left her at a final five foot four. She read recently that she had reached the exact height of the average American woman. Marylou had achieved normalcy, but the damage was done.

Now thirty, she was proud of the ownership she was taking of her past and self-growth. One of her coping tactics was seeking out smaller friends in an attempt to break the cycle of social derision she assumed all short people experienced. Pammy was her smallest friend yet, but something had been off-balance lately. Marylou was sure it was just a phase; all friendships morphed and shifted, and Pammy had her size to deal with on top of the normal challenges.

She had recently started attending a support group at a local church to learn to cope with her insecurities. Three months into these weekly sessions, she felt she'd come a long way.

But today, after the group had gone around the circle with customary greetings and introductions, she felt the intimidating beam of the spotlight.

"Marylou, we all talked after you left last week, and we wanted to bring some things up," said Sharon, an outspoken older woman with grown children and horrific but often hilarious tales of her battle with alcoholism.

"Okay…" said Marylou cautiously. *Talked after I left? Was that even allowed?*

"We know we're not therapists, but we have concerns about your friendship with Pammy."

Marylou's face flushed as she saw the other heads nodding in agreement. "Meaning?" she asked, her eyebrows raised defensively.

"We all believe that Pammy is dangerous. We feel we

need to inform your family if you are not willing to deal with her, so that someone knows what is going on."

Marylou looked around the room at the sober faces. Smirking, she said, "Dangerous? You're joking, right? She is my best friend and she gets a kick out of playing pranks. You're blowing it out of proportion."

Sharon was clearly elected to speak on behalf of the group. "Honey, we know you have worked hard to shed old resentments and recognize your very average size. We think the next step is to end this friendship with your mini-friend."

At the word "mini," Marylou cringed. She hated that childish label. Minis were as varied and unique as any normal-sized human, but the accepted social stereotype was that they were mean and aggressive.

"Sweetheart, let me offer you another perspective." This came from Ron, an oily man who rarely talked about himself and seemed to be here just for his own weird version of entertainment. "You've tried to fix your past through relationships with short people, one after the other, and through Pammy most of all. But she is just a troublemaker who is bringing you more anxiety than happiness. You can't see that because you want so badly to believe *she* needs *you*."

Marylou stared blankly.

"We can see you're having some trouble with this, honey," said Bev, the gentle, overweight woman next to her, as she patted her knee. "The main point here is that the last story you told us about Pammy hiding in your shower and then spraying your eyes with pepper spray was the final straw for us. That is simply not a normal prank."

"But it was April Fool's Day!" Marylou said desperately.

"Is that how she justified it? Oh, no. No, no, no." Sharon shook her head vigorously.

Marylou lashed out. "You guys don't get it. If you have friends like Pammy, you are responsible for them. You just can't relate because you don't have any small friends. People are careless. If you don't pay attention, they could actually die, just like Randy Newman wanted!"

"He didn't actually mean physically short people, you know. And it's just a song," said a younger, long-haired man she decided was too filthy to actually listen to. She never could remember his name.

"Songs have power, and he should have been more careful. He almost ruined my life!" Marylou could feel herself falling apart. "Besides, you just don't know Pammy. She has a dark sense of humor."

"It's not just dark. It's sick, and you are her target," Bev declared.

This was more than Marylou could process. It was true, Pammy had started to be more devilish in her pranks. Sometimes Marylou even felt scared, which she'd never admit to these people. As they droned on, citing examples to pound the point home, she tuned them out and drifted back to the events that had led her here.

*****

For years, Marylou and Pammy had relied on each other as companions for travel adventures that sisters and boyfriends weren't interested in having. The execution of these trips was always a bit rocky, given Pammy's size. Most people didn't know how to behave around someone eight inches tall.

A few years back, they had gone on a hut-to-hut trek through the Alps. Near the end of a day of hiking, which they had expected to take three hours but had actually already taken six, Marylou was wiped out. She had met some friendly trekkers in the final stretch and enjoyed chatting with them to pass the time. What she hadn't noticed with her new distraction was that Pammy had fallen from her lookout spot on top of the rolled sleep sacks and into the backpack. As Marylou hiked, Pammy was bounced farther and farther down to the bottom, tormented by Marylou and her new friends singing "My Favorite Things," John Denver, Neil Diamond.

When they finally arrived, Marylou was damp with sweat and measurably filthy wherever trail dust had found wet skin. Upon entering the hut, she was immediately confronted by a bouncy, fresh-faced young woman who introduced herself as Sarah and bombarded Marylou with a soliloquy about the house rules.

"Hi! Welcome! Did you have a good day? Did you take the valley route or the vista route? We took the valley route and it was beautiful but long. Where are you from? Really? SoCal? Cool! I'm Sarah, I'm from NorCal! You can put your poles and boots in that room over there. No shoes allowed inside the hut. Showers are downstairs and to the left. You need a token to take a shower. Each token gives you about two and a half minutes. If you want two tokens you can buy them but don't be greedy with the hot water. Dinner is at seven, and everybody eats together."

Marylou forced a grin. "Do you work here?"

"No no. Just a trekker, like you. Are you traveling with anyone?"

It was at that moment that Marylou realized she had forgotten about Pammy. She excused herself and stepped away. She whipped her pack around and started to dig, frantically throwing out her clothes and energy bars.

"Pammy! Pammy!"

Her companion was smashed between a moist plum pit and a pair of dirty wool socks. As soon as Marylou raised her out of the pack, Pammy threw up.

"Oh my god, I'm so sorry! How long have you been down there?"

"You don't even know. Wow. Fuck you." Pammy attempted to spit in Marylou's direction, but it wasn't an effective amount.

"I *don't* know. Please don't talk like that. It was a long day, and I was distracted at the end. My knees ache. I'm so hungry."

"Oh, wow, poor you. We came on this trip together, remember? I'm not one of the inanimate things in your backpack," she snarled.

"I'm glad you're okay," Marylou said honestly.

"How about you don't talk to me," Pammy said, pulling plum pulp from her hair. "Can I please get to a shower?"

"Sure," Marylou said. Of course she felt bad, but she expected a little gratitude and forgiveness. It's not like Pammy would have been able to do this on her own. Marylou grabbed their shower supplies and took Pammy to the communal washroom.

Marylou dropped in the shower tokens, and Pammy waited on the soap shelf for Marylou to rinse her with water collected in the shampoo cap. They went back to their room and dressed, but the mood was awkward. Pammy was running a plastic spork through her wet hair when Marylou broke the silence.

"Are you coming to dinner?"

"I guess. I have to eat." Pammy sat comfortably with her grudges.

"I could bring you something, but I'd rather you come with me." Marylou was determined to get things back on track.

"Fine," Pammy said, not at all warmly.

Dinner wasn't ready, so Marylou ordered a beer at the front desk and they went outside to the stone patio to enjoy the view. She sat at the end of a long bench, and Pammy climbed up into a small pot of bright red geraniums, which gave her a better vantage point while still disguising her.

As Marylou took her first sip, Sarah and the rest of her NorCal gang entered and took over the other end of the table. Marylou sighed and tried to avoid eye contact, but Sarah did not pick up on the cue.

"Hey, SoCal! All cleaned up! Got your beer?"

"Yup." Marylou held it up in an air toast.

Because she and Pammy weren't speaking, it was impossible not to eavesdrop on the NorCal conversation. It was nice hearing English speakers talking about her home state, and she was feeling lighter and blissfully buzzed. She interjected here and there, and soon was actually enjoying their company.

Mid-discussion of the best campsites in Yosemite, she reached too casually for her beer, and backhanded Pammy off her perch and headfirst into the mug. Pammy kicked wildly, splashing beer everywhere. Suddenly, the entire table was silent and staring at them. Marylou grabbed her friend by the ankle, lifted her out, and wiped her face.

Stunned and not prepared to explain Pammy to the group, she left the table without a word. She was embarrassed by her negligence, but even more by the very existence of Pammy, and this made her feel terrible. They did not speak the rest of the night. Marylou hadn't realized it at the time, but now she knew that had been the turning point in their friendship. She'd awakened the next morning with several tiny bites all over her torso, some of which had drawn blood. She'd expected a Pammy temper-tantrum, but the violence was new.

They finished the final few days of their trip in silence. Once home, Pammy became more and more of a menace. One day, Marylou found mice crawling all over the apartment through holes in the wall, which Pammy admitted she'd dug out with a knife and filled with bits of food scraps. The next day, thumbtacks "accidentally" spilled on the floor right by Marylou's bedside.

When Marylou confronted her, Pammy simply laughed. Then the pepper spray incident occurred. She knew it had been a step too far, and yet life without her friend, her shorter friend...

*****

"Hello? Marylou? Are you listening to us at all?"

She snapped back to attention and looked around the room at the group.

"Yes, yes, I'm listening."

"Has any of this sunk in? Are you seeing what we're seeing? You are choosing to let your friend hurt you. We're afraid she might do permanent damage."

"I don't know. I thought she needed me...but maybe I misread it."

"That's for sure. Sadistic pranks are rarely a sign of a healthy friendship," said the filthy guy.

Marylou sighed. "I have a lot to think about. Give me a week before you say anything. I will deal with it."

As she walked out, Sharon called after her, "Take care of yourself. We're going to check on you and see how it went."

Marylou left, knowing she'd never be back. *Grubby little fingers, dirty little minds....* The more she thought about Pammy, the angrier she got. Had she or had she not saved Pammy's life several times? Hiked days through the Alps despite bleeding ankles and wrapped knees, while that ungrateful urchin enjoyed the view? Taken her out into a mean, harsh world where she could never have ventured on her own? Newman was right, but he hadn't been talking *about* Marylou at all; he had been talking *to* her. It had been a warning. *They're gonna get you every time....*

Smiling, she thought, *nope. Not gonna get me.* Nobody would miss Pammy, that rat. For all anyone would know, she could be lost in Costco. They wouldn't look for her long. They never did, as minis were rarely recovered. *"Don't want no short people, don't want no short people 'round here..."* she sang quietly to herself. It was funny how things changed.

Passports

It seemed strange to Alice that she felt more herself when she traveled. It made her wonder if she applied a veneer to her "real" life. How much was a cover story and how much was actually her? Away from home, there was no one around telling her that she was self-assured, that her convictions were strong, that she was decisive—a natural leader. She knew this was what she evoked. But there was freedom in the vulnerability she was feeling now, in the doubt and indecision that accompanied travel. She felt raw and honest.

She also felt sunburned, having spent the last three days on her search for old French ivory knives. Her parents had always wanted to come to France and bought the tickets as soon as they retired then invited her to come along. Maybe that was why she was feeling more vulnerable, she considered, her dynamic with them made her constantly feel unsure of herself, that anything she'd adopted as a perspective or belief after she'd turned eighteen was the cause of some nefarious group who had brainwashed her. University professors, dorm-mates, people in the big city where she now lived—and where they never liked to visit. Her parents didn't recognize her as a wholly independent person.

"I have the passports with me," her mother stated as she folded her dirty napkin, as though someone had asked.

"The hotel safe is safe." Her dad grinned at Alice, satisfied with his wordplay. He'd allowed his wine glass to be refilled one time too many at lunch, which caused lapses in his sense of humor.

"That barely counts as a pun, Dad."

He snorted, nonetheless pleased with himself.

"Mom, if you are going to carry them in your purse, just wear it inside your jacket. I agree with Dad; you should have left them at the hotel."

"I don't trust the cleaning crew. None of them are even French. Now, what's our plan for the afternoon?"

Alice let her mother's offensive comment slide. She hadn't traveled much, Alice reminded herself, and watched way too much cable news. Having the knife mission had actually been a nice focus for them, a way to avoid the nagging travel talk about meal-timing and blisters…and non-European staff. The trio stepped out of the restaurant and into a cold rain that suddenly spilled from the sky. It stung then soothed her sunburned shoulders, but her mother shrieked as though she were under gunfire.

"Let's get inside somewhere! Hurry!" her mom yelled, holding a guidebook over her head. Alice glanced around at the options and considered where she'd most like to be stranded. There was the café right there, but she was tired of sitting and making chit-chat. She scanned: a pharmacy, a pre-school, and just beyond that, a second-hand shop.

"Over there, the shop!" she called to her parents.

They darted inside the dilapidated, centuries-old building. The shop was musty and the goods were caked with layers of dust. *Why even be in this line of business if you don't take care of these things?* she wondered. There were actually some cool pieces if you could stand the odor and grime. The air was almost foggy.

"Help me look for the knives, would you?" She coaxed her parents from their spot just inside the door.

Alice wandered through the small rooms, eventually coming to a cordoned-off display case that seemed promising. She blew the dust away, which created an overpowering smell that swirled around her head and made her cough. Sunshine broke through clouds, entered a tiny window, and lit up the room. Alice squinted toward the light and could see an older man outside, gnawing on a cigar and having what seemed to be a dramatic argument with a couple. They handed him something, then got into a van parked just outside the shop.

"Honey, no luck for me," her dad said, fewer than five minutes after entering the store. "I'll wait outside." This was no surprise. Her father hated old things; he'd never bought a used item in his life. He'd rather be soaking wet than in here. Or back in the café continuing to feed his wine buzz.

Alice looked around for her mother. She saw her walking toward the back of the store on the hunt. *Such a good sport*, Alice thought and smiled.

She rubbed her eyes. When she pulled her hands away from her face, the older, overweight man stood in front of her with his stinking cigar.

"You looking something?"

Based on his English, she doubted her ability to communicate her knife needs to him.

"I help you? Need souvenir?"

"Sure…uh…I'm looking for knives. French ivory? Do you have any?"

He stared blankly at her. She tried again.

"Knives, for cutting?" she sawed at an imaginary steak.

He put his hand on her shoulder and leaned closer.

"You. Brown hair girl. Brown eye."

"What?" She wished she were less polite and could shoo his hand away, but she was distracted by her burning eyes and squeezed them closed again.

"About twenty-five year old? Maybe thirty?" he pressed.

She reached for her water bottle. She felt woozy. As she unscrewed the top, she looked for her mother.

"Mom? Ready to go?" she called out in no particular direction, suddenly wishing she had followed her dad.

Hearing no reply, she walked past the man, whose exhalations of cigar smoke were not helping the air quality. "Mom?" she called again.

She worked her way through the store, the shopkeeper on her heels.

Alice got to the back of the shop and was stunned to see her mother sitting on the floor, leaning against the wall, her legs straight out in front of her, a blank stare on her face.

"Mom!"

On the floor next to her, a petite older woman was squatting, rifling through her mom's purse with no attempt at discretion. Her mom was within arm's reach of the woman but did nothing to stop her. She didn't even react to what was happening.

"Mom? Did you fall? What are you doing with her bag?!" Alice lunged toward the woman, but the shopkeeper, who was again at her side, grabbed Alice first. She tried to jerk away but he held tight. She turned back to her mom, alarmed. "MOM! What happened?" Then to the woman, "Give that to me, that's hers!"

She tried to pull away from the man, but her body would not cooperate. She felt herself collapse to the floor, first her knees then her torso. The floor smacked her left cheekbone as her right arm was pinned beneath her ribcage.

Alice looked up and barely made out the fuzzy form of the lady holding up all of their passports. She handed them to the shopkeeper, who promptly disappeared down a hallway. She looked back at her mom, whose eyes had now shut, then back toward the hall. She faintly heard his voice say, "I have a match, your lucky day!" followed by a muffled expression of delight. "You give me money, you go soon," he continued. *Who? Go where?* Alice wondered as her eyes fell closed.

*****

Feeling rejuvenated by the rain and fresh air, Alice's father was becoming impatient. What in the world were they doing? The shop was not that large. He turned the brass knob on the shop door, but now it was locked. *That's odd,* he thought. He peered through the small window in the door, covered with so much grime that he could just barely make out the image of his wife and daughter lying on the floor.

"Hey! Open up! Honey! Alice! Can you hear me?" He banged on the door, but no one else was in sight. He ran to the side of the building, desperate to get someone's attention. A voice called from behind the house. "Got any more? Van's leaving!" The old lady yelled out the back door: "Just few minute! We have more for you today!"

Her father banged on the window again. "Hey! Lady! Open the door! Let me in now!" She glanced in his direction, emotionless, and turned away. He barely caught the reflection of the shopkeeper before he felt a crushing whack on his skull.

The New Gig

It was more jarring than scary at first. Lucy had just finished a marathon session on her computer at her local coffee joint and was feeling pretty clever. She was on fire, at least as far as the social media universe was concerned, slinging witty and well-researched accusations about her cause du jour, which was the local cocaine epidemic in her city that had spiked when she was still in college a few years back. After digging herself out of her own powdery hell—a hell that so many young people tumbled into around here and from which many never returned—she had found a way to merge her experience and skills, forging a path toward a respectable career.

She'd successfully situated herself as the primary voice attacking the local law enforcement response rather than joining the throngs going after the dealers and the shady overlords. Lucy had a natural tendency to resist authority and the most commonly accepted notions about good guys and bad guys. As a young girl, her mom labeled her difficult, and lately she wondered if she simply felt compelled to fulfill a maternal prophecy.

It was a lean living, but with a journalism degree, there wasn't much waiting for her in the work-a-day world anyway. There was a decent network of local and national regulars debating the epidemic, and she was right in the mix, though nearly alone on her side of the aisle. The quantity of retweets and shares validated her decisions even when they came from trolls and haters. Today had been a banner day in that regard.

Once the coffee buzz overcame her productivity, she paid the tab and packed her laptop. The bright sun made her squint as she tried to fit the key in the door of her Jetta, when suddenly there was a hand gripping the back of her neck. Instinctually she tried to turn around, but her head was pushed forward so her chin hit her chest, making it difficult for her to breathe.

She was redirected to a nearby sedan. She heard shuffling feet around her. She couldn't see the people they belonged to, but she confirmed from the small vantage point under her armpit that there were at least three of them, and based on their shoes, she was pretty sure they were men.

"What's your home address? Your first home."

"Where I grew up? My mother's home? Why?"

"What is it?" came the firm reply, delivered with an accent that brought to mind her recent obsession with the Mexican actor Gael Garcia Bernal.

She rattled off the address of the home she hadn't lived in

for years as if she'd never left, which always surprised her. She racked her brain trying to remember her mom's schedule and where she might possibly be. Zumba was after dinner…what day did she volunteer at the library? The coffee was making her brain jumpy.

"Why are we going there? Are you going to hurt my mom?"

"There shouldn't be any reason to do that, should there, Lucia?" The hand belonging to the voice gave her a hearty thump on the shoulder. "We aren't violent. Do we seem violent?"

Hearing her name escalated her panic. She was being targeted? Why? She tried to calm down. She remembered from debate club that in an antagonistic situation it was important to display strength and self-confidence. She could start there.

"Well, I obviously don't know anything about you," she said matter-of-factly, then after a pause added, "How do you know me?"

"No more questions."

They drove for the better part of an hour, and with each passing minute Lucy's fear battled her inner resolve to get through this. Her mind scanned all the mistakes she'd made in the past and questioned whether this was one of those coming back to haunt her. By the time they turned into the driveway where she once played tetherball, her body was in a permanent state of tension; she was aware of even the smallest muscles around her temples and along her throat. She closed her eyes and said a prayer that the house would be empty.

No such luck. They barged into the kitchen through the side door, which had been left wide open, Lucy being guided forcefully by her neck. The first thing she saw was her mom.

"Lucy!"

Lucy's heart pounded as she stared at the ground. She couldn't bear the look of disappointment, even disgust, that she was sure she'd see on her mother's face. She could feel the modicum of respect that she had finally earned disintegrating. Lucy was once again just a child who caused her mother pain.

She looked around to see things as her mom saw them. She was embarrassed that the first thing that struck her was how *attractive* her kidnappers were. She saw a young, slight man with a hairstyle that clearly required some effort—his thick, wavy, dark locks were gelled into a state of hipness. His posture suggested he was compensating for his lack of experience; his shoulders were held back just a little too far, his upper arms and elbows fell unnaturally behind him rather than at his side. In training, she figured.

"What's happening, Lucy?" her mother asked as she watched the parade of men escort her daughter across the kitchen. But all Lucy heard was: *what have you done now?*

"I don't know—"

The man who had done all the talking so far cut her off. "Just keep cooking that meal, *señora*. Everything will be fine. It smells fantastic." Then, to the third man who was still holding Lucy by the neck, "Sit her down over there." He indicated the kitchen table. This one was clearly the ringleader, though an unlikely one. He seemed like a guy who would be on a minor league soccer team, maybe even the one they'd put on the billboards advertising their games. His hair fell in loose rings of curls around his face, and he wore a fitted athletic sweatshirt with a collar, zipped to the top, and trendy orange sneakers.

She was pushed into the chair by the last man, who released her but remained standing uncomfortably close. She took him in from her periphery. He was the biggest and possibly oldest of the three, but still no more than thirty-five. He seemed to be the muscle of the group, tall and beefy, with a small tattoo of a butterfly on his neck. He communicated only with head movements.

Lucy made mental notes in case she needed to describe them later. She tried to reconcile their attractiveness with the fact that they had kidnapped her—a crime that had violent potential. Her throat constricted.

"We want to employ you," said Curly.

She didn't respond right away as she realized she might now have a shred of power. "Employ me as what? You need another kidnapper?" Sarcasm could seem like strength, she reasoned. It drew an alarmed glance from her mother at the stove but it did nothing to rattle Curly. She noticed his green eyes and broad shoulders.

"We are not kidnappers. We are not thugs. We are employed by the HBJ cartel."

"The Mexican drug cartel? Why are you here? And why would I want to work for criminals?"

"Business is good here. Thriving, not violent. Yet. But we need to know how things work—who knows what, where we stand. That's why we want you. You have an audience, you can change perceptions, draw attention away from certain areas...certain people."

This was not an outcome she had imagined. She had fantasized in the past that the local public radio station or newspaper may notice her work and that she may be able to leverage that into a job. She had interviewed countless people that were affected by drugs—addicts, witnesses to crimes, victims of police busts that were shady. But to be noticed by the cartel? Lucy's mind reeled.

Trainee, his chin thrust forward, offered a taunt. "You write about us. You're interested, admit it." He rocked back and forth from foot to foot and spoke with a nervous energy. Curly shot him a look, and he shut up.

"We read your blog and follow you on Twitter." Curly moved slowly toward her. "We know that you can help us throw undesirables off our trail, craft a new narrative, write a new story *para nosotros*. Think of it as a promotion. New *jefes, aventura, la vida buena. Habla español, no?*"

He was now directly behind her chair. He gripped her shoulders and looked up at her mother. "Don't you want your daughter to have success, *mama?*" His heavy hands lingered on Lucy's shoulders. She hated herself for feeling a slight melting sensation.

"*Bueno*. Lucia, you will be put up in a loft downtown. All your expenses covered, plus a hundred grand U.S. We will monitor all your movements. If you leave to meet someone, visit the *mercado*, use the *baño*, we will know about it."

Her mother fumbled with a pan at the stove. As it began to dawn on her she'd been handpicked due to her work, she felt slightly less fearful and more hopeful about her chances to get safely through this. *Maybe this isn't so bad. An undercover journalist! And paid well. A lot more than those poor slobs I graduated with at those local dailies in those shithole towns, earning nickels. Play the hand you're dealt.*

"Okay, but I have a question."

"Which is?"

"What's the point of involving my mom? Why did we come here?"

Her mother looked up from the stove, but as soon as she caught Curly's eye she looked away again. He was working his thumbs deep into Lucy's shoulder muscles. It was destabilizing; she shivered. He leaned in and spoke softly into her ear.

"Collateral."

Then, standing up, he continued. "Jaime will be staying here with your mother." He nodded at Butterfly, who remained silent. "Insurance that you don't…disappoint us, shall we say."

She watched her mom, but instead of feeling guilt for the situation she was putting her in, all she could think about was this man behind her. She found herself wondering if he might visit her at her loft.

Her mother looked at her with a fearful, furrowed brow, her eyes gathering water. Lucy knew that her mom had never understood her choices. Why should things change now? It would all work out.

Lucy rose from her chair. Butterfly sat down in her place as if he expected dinner to be served, and Curly and Trainee flanked her on both sides. She walked toward her mother and kissed her on the cheek without saying a word then calmly walked out of the house.

Tourist Trap

"Fuck guidebooks!" That was the tall one's operating principal. She and her travel partner, best friends since college Spanish, prided themselves on staying away from places other people raved about in Lonely Planet or Frommers. So here they were, off the beaten path in this little town, wandering around the streets with not much to do. They hoped to meet some people over a beer and then call it a day. They preferred the company of locals, but even the most dedicated wanderers enjoyed an occasional evening now and then with kindred adventurers to share battle stories and find out where to get a drink in the next town.

"You girls having a good time here?"

A man appeared out of nowhere. His type, though creepy, was familiar to them: an unofficial town ambassador looking for a quick buck.

"We are, thanks. It's a cute town," the tall brunette answered in the local tongue. She regretted the use of 'cute' immediately. That was unlikely to translate the way she intended.

"Where are you from?"

"We're from the States," said the other girl, short and blonde, in a southern drawl.

"Ahh, America. We don't get a lot of you. Australians, Germans, yes, but not you." He had casually, and without invitation, joined them on their walk.

"Well, maybe that's why we like it here!" They laughed at the idea that no one wanted to be around Americans, even Americans themselves.

He shook his head. "We love Americans here. Very friendly people, and fun. Do you girls want to have some fun?"

"We're having fun right now." The tall one was naturally cynical, and this was sounding like a sales pitch.

"I mean something unique. You know of the prison, of course? For which we are...infamous?"

Yes, they knew. It was the only significant thing about this town, and the only reason tourists ever came here. Many political prisoners had been held there during a civil war decades ago, and most had never made it out.

"Yes, we know about it."

"Well," he leaned forward and said quietly, "you can sleep overnight in a cell. Cheap."

"No thank you!" The southerner gave a visible shudder. "Do people really do that?"

"It's quite an experience. People enjoy it very much. There are several other visitors staying tonight."

The girls exchanged a look that solidified their agreement. "We don't want to sleep there, but maybe we'll check it out."

"It's just down this street. I'll take you there. Once you see it you'll change your minds."

They walked with him down a cobblestone street, past mostly abandoned stucco storefronts and a man in a tank top selling bottles of Coca-Cola through a sliding window. After a few short blocks, they arrived at a plain, unmarked cinder block structure.

"So is this it?" Their tone revealed their curiosity just enough for him to drag them a little farther along.

He nodded. "Come, I'll show you the rooms."

"We told you we're not staying, we just want to have a look."

In one quick motion, he turned to face them, and the tall one could now see loose tobacco leaves stuck between his yellowed teeth. "Prisoners do not get to decide whether they stay, not even in America, do they?" His sinister delivery was betrayed only by an exaggerated lift of one eyebrow, which they chalked up to part of his act.

The tall one laughed to lighten the mood. "No, you're right, they don't. We already have plans for the night, but thanks for bringing us here. Where does everyone hang out?" She reached into her pocket to find the appropriate coin for a tip.

"Follow me."

The short one scrunched her face into a grimace as she looked at her friend. They entered, and he led them down the cellblock corridor until the fading sun gave way to the windowless darkness. Clicking on a small flashlight he pulled from his pocket, he illuminated the handle of a cell door. The room was excessively simple, with only a thin sheet on the bed and a light bulb dangling above.

"What was the inspiration? Eighties USSR-chic?" said the brunette, under her breath.

The man ignored her, stepped out, and pulled the door closed. They started to protest, but he pushed it back open to indicate it wasn't locked, grinning. As he walked away, he announced, "Your comrades are at the end of this corridor to the left, if you feel like joining them for a drink at the bar. Enjoy, and bang if you need anything."

Once he was safely out of earshot, the short one turned to her friend.

"Okay, this is weird. Did he not understand that we aren't staying? He's freaking me out."

"No idea. Let's go to the bar and talk to some people."

They let themselves out of the cell and walked in the direction of a low din, which grew louder as they approached. Around a corner, they came upon a common area, complete with a pool table and a bar, and several young people. They brightened a bit.

Once they got close enough for the crowd to see them, the talking stopped immediately. The inhabitants eyed the newcomers and began speaking in hushed tones in the local tongue. The girls realized these weren't tourists at all. It was as if the scene were staged.

"Hu-uh. This isn't right. Let's go back," said the tall one.

"Yeah. Now."

Before they could walk out, two of the bar patrons grabbed the tall girl's elbows and sat her on a barstool.

"What are you doing? Let go!" She tried to twist her way out of their grips but they held firm.

The short one turned her head to see what was happening, then smelled the particular scent of moist tobacco. She spun around and was face to face with their host.

"You aren't pleased with the accommodations?" he asked.

"We just wanted a beer," she said, trying to maintain the courtesies of a guest.

"Is that what you want? I want something too."

"What is going on?" demanded the tall one. "We're leaving."

"I don't care what *you* do. Boys, she's all yours." Then he turned to the short one. "*You* are staying, and I'll be having my way with you."

The tall one lunged from her stool in a last ditch effort to get away before being pulled back down and held in place. She watched helplessly as the man closed in on her friend from behind and grabbed her around the waist.

Terror pierced her yell. "What kind of place is this?! You expect tourists to come here if you play these games with them?"

"I can assure you this is not a game," he whispered into his captive's ear. "Surely you are familiar with tourist traps. We are so grateful for your patronage."

He picked her up from behind, pinning her arms to her sides, and backed out the door toward the dark cellblock, overpowering her attempts to kick and buck herself free. She called out for help, but the locals just went back to their drinks.

Part 3
Coming Soon

*"I feel a frantic desire to free myself.
To start all over again and in another way."*
– Milan Kundera

Sosche

Hillary had never been in a building like this one. She glanced around the lobby one last time as the elevator shut, sealing them into an airtight compartment. She and six strangers rode in silence to the 103rd floor, and she considered whether humans were meant to live this far above the earth. But times change, she acknowledged, and this was the apartment of the future. She didn't want to be left behind like some Luddite. She'd been to college, sure, but her first twenty five years had mostly been spent living in a conservative small town. She'd never even done any real traveling. *Well, you're in the big city now. Time to open your eyes to new possibilities.*

At least she had Monica, her childhood friend from the neighborhood. They had witnessed each other's awkward high school years and had survived the bad haircuts and suspect boyfriends together. They'd even shared a college apartment in the mid-2020s.

Monica had moved here three years ago and responded so positively to it she'd convinced Hillary to move here, too. Hillary figured she could live with Monica again, and it'd be good to have someone to show her the ropes. It was expensive compared to home and that worried Hillary, but Monica said the more people who rented, the cheaper it would be, which was why she was trying to recruit friends and co-workers.

She had also mentioned it was a non-traditional living arrangement, but Hillary didn't press about what that meant. Non-traditional meant current to her, and that was good because she was done with traditional, which she now felt meant out-of-touch. Change was what she was after. Maybe the other roommates had exotic pets. That would be okay with her as long as they weren't ferrets or some other equally filthy creature. She knew someone who had a hedgehog, and it was actually pretty cute. She would keep her mind open.

The elevator coasted to a graceful stop, and the doors silently parted. She looked to her right and saw a long concrete lobby lined with sofas and artwork; to her left, a glistening bathroom. Finally, her eyes found Monica.

"You're like a lost doe! Relax! You made it!" Monica reached out for her, and Hillary accepted the familiar but uncomfortable shoulders-only embrace of her friend. Some people just weren't huggers.

"Where are your bags?" Monica asked.

"I left them in the lobby. Just wanted to figure out where I was going first."

"Good idea. Hope you didn't bring much! This is us right

here."

Monica walked her down through the lobby and eventually to a living area with a sparkling kitchen off to one side. The appliances were Jetson-like with no visible buttons or dials or even digital interfaces—truly top-of-the-line. Hillary started to feel excited; she was finally moving into a brand new chapter of her life. Monica raced around pointing out feature after feature then came to a small area with a bed separated from the living space by a partial acrylic glass wall, which was illustrated with projected digital information.

HILLARY CROWLEY. 28 YO. SOCIAL ID: UNPARTNERED, CAUCASIAN (INCOMPLETE DATA). PREFERRED CLIMATE: 74 DEGREES. REQUESTED QUIET HOURS: 11:30P – 7A. DIETARY RESTRICTIONS: DAIRY INTOLERANT. PETS: NONE. DEFAULT MOOD: PENSIVE.

"Here's your area!"

"I can see that!" She did not remember providing this information. "Where's yours?"

"Just behind the wine fridge. See my data wall?"

"Oh just right there? So, this is what they call a double?"

Monica smiled as if at a child. "Yes. Two beds." She

pointed at each for emphasis.

Hillary hated the way Monica could patronize her in just subtle enough a way that she could deny she was doing it. It made her feel inadequate, naïve. She vowed to not let her disappointment be detected. She could adjust to this…bed…space, she told herself. She'd get used to it after awhile, just like anything. She bounced back. "Okay, cool. So where's the bathroom? I'm dying to pee."

"It's that way. Toward the elevator." Monica was distracted by the flickering lights of a changing data wall nearby and merely waved Hillary in the general direction of the entry as she walked away.

"Thanks. Be right back." The enthusiasm she tried to work up wasn't at all authentic, and she wondered if Monica could tell. She would need to get better at hiding her feelings in the city.

She looked for the bathroom but didn't find it where she expected to. Instead, she wandered farther until she was pretty sure she wasn't in their apartment anymore. The only bathroom she saw was the one she'd noticed when she got off the elevator. She doubled back toward the kitchen, figuring she missed it. She pivoted again and found herself back at the elevator. This time she noticed that there was no actual door—just a doorframe. A man walked out wiping his hands on his jeans. He nodded a greeting to her as he passed then went straight into the elevator only feet away.

This must be the lobby bathroom, Hillary thought. *Better than nothing.* She went inside, and there were a half a dozen stalls. It was sleek and modern, and the door on each extended all the way to the floor providing some privacy. Still, she couldn't help feeling weird that a strange man might be next to her. The urgency passed, and she walked out.

"Hey," Monica greeted her while stirring honey into her tea. "Feeling better?"

"Yeah. But I never found our bathroom. I went to the main one by the elevator."

"Yeah, the one you walked past when you came up? That's the one I was talking about."

"So is that *our* bathroom? Cause I saw a guy walk out of it...is he a friend of yours?"

"I don't know, but yes, it's ours. And his, and whoever's. Shared."

Hillary paused, waiting for further explanation, and when it never came, she said, "So we don't have our own bathroom. Got it. I'm gonna walk around, check the rest of the place out."

"Yes, explore!" said Monica.

"Cool. I'll be right back."

She was no prude, but it was nice to sit on a toilet without someone right next to you, man or woman, wall or not. She couldn't imagine that she was the only one here who felt that way.

She found herself in an open space encircled by dozens of data walls flickering with information. She walked by a living space with a guy slouched on a couch engaged in a virtual reality adventure. She continued on, seeing a young woman sleeping in a bed-area much like hers.

Eventually she came to an area covered with green shag recycled plastic rugs, along with several dogs and their respective owners. The animals were milling about and sniffing each other. She almost admonished one indifferent owner, who was self-involved in a hologram soccer game playing inches in front of his face and didn't seem to notice when his poodle lifted a leg all over one of the rugs. As soon as the dog was done, the guy—never looking away from the game—picked up the rug and tossed it into a bin. Then he reached over to a stack of similar rugs, threw a new one down, and continued his stroll.

Moving on, she saw a man sitting down to eat in boxer shorts then heard a couple arguing about their relationship status displayed on their data wall.

"Why does yours suddenly say quad-partnered?"

"We talked about this! Josef and Adrian are with us now."

"No! I agreed to fool around, but not to quad-partner! And you put it on our *wall*? Not okay!"

Hillary stepped away quickly, but others lingered outside watching it unfold, and yet the arguing didn't stop.

She made it back and approached Monica, who was curled up comfortably with her tea.

"So what is the deal with this place?" she blurted out.

"What do you mean, 'the deal'?"

Monica made this sound like a ridiculous question. Hillary's face heated up. Before she could respond, two young women rollerbladed right between them, the plastic wheels whirring along the shiny floor.

She whipped her head around to Monica. "Okay, who are they?" she demanded.

"I don't know, they live here!" She waved her hands wildly over her head to indicate the general vicinity.

"Does it matter?"

"Yeah, Monica, it does. Where does our apartment start and stop? There was a man in our bathroom. Two women you don't know just cruised through our conversation! Why are you acting like these are weird questions?"

Monica smirked. "Okay, I guess I shouldn't be that surprised. You haven't heard of Sosche-Space. You know, as in social spaces? They are basically socially-engineered, shared condos. Like the dating websites from years ago. It makes so much more sense! The buildings have profiles that match you up with similar people. I mean, we're not all exactly alike, but we have at least some things in common—our interests, our style, our fashion sense, our politics. So much better than the old-fashioned way of letting anyone live anywhere they want. What a mess! Remember the Tildens who lived at the end of the street when we were little? They hated kids! We hated them! It made no sense for us to be neighbors. And the freaks that moved in next door to us in that shithole apartment in college? They were doing séances and selling dream catchers! We didn't belong with them. I shouldn't have to experience that, and now I don't!"

She spread her arms out, as if she were Willy Wonka showing off his factory.

"Look around. We have dozens of showers to choose

from, with different tile patterns and various shower heads. Pulsing, rain shower, anything you want. Or look for a tub that has your favorite bath oil next to it. Different sofas to sit on when we get tired of this one. But all in a style that suits us! It's easy to meet people; no more isolation or lonely nights. Every city is going to start copying this. You know how bad you feel when you don't get a reply to a post for a few hours? You're like, 'Where did everybody go? Are they sleeping in today? Are they having dinner and I wasn't invited?' It used to make me crazy! I mean, almost everyone I know was spending all their money on therapists, feeling alienated and less-than. And since we were posting about where we were all the time anyway, the next natural step was that we all just started congregating in the same places at the same time. Now you don't wait to hear from anyone, you just walk into any dinner party that looks good and sit down! No more hard choices, no more hurt feelings. It's brilliant!"

Hillary absorbed all of this. Then with an emotionless face, she turned and walked toward her bed. She curled up on top of the fluffy white comforter. Monica was right: this was the kind of comforter she would have chosen for herself, probably at Pottery Barn.

She lay on her side, curled into a fetal position, and closed her eyes, imagining the walls growing toward the ceiling. The Tildens had seemed like crotchety old people when she was a kid, but she'd run into them as an adult and actually found them pretty interesting. What was being decided for her, removed from her life, that she'd never know? She heard someone walk past and sensed that person looking at her, there in her bed. She heard the cacophony of television sets, conversations, and barking dogs, all competing to fill any empty pockets of silence that might still exist.

She plugged her ears and started to cry.

Department Store

Taylor took a deep breath and turned off her car. *You made it*, she said to herself. *The last day. Cheer up!* She grabbed her keys and looked up at the department store, cursing the bright sun that reflected off the car windshields and the specks in the concrete, causing her to squint.

As soon as she stepped out of the car, a plastic bag blowing across the baking cement brushed the tops of her sandaled feet. The intense summer heat had spread a sense of abandonment across her town. Indeed, most of the people would escape to cooler places on this oppressive day, and many would come here: this huge, air-conditioned, windowless department store—a magnet for hope, consumption, and deceit. Taylor kicked the plastic bag, and it flew softly into the air. As it floated down, she kicked it again. The small buckle on her sandal caught the handle of the bag, and her hysterical attempts to free it were futile. She grabbed the bag off her foot violently and ripped it in half. She looked around to see if anyone had seen the scuffle. Then she turned again toward the gigantic structure in front of her.

When Taylor was a young girl, she had always looked forward to coming here. The overwhelming racks of clothes, purses, and the endless cases of jewelry excited her. The music was magical: the right song that she'd forgotten how much she once loved always came on at just the right time, and a pleasant euphoria would wash over her, spurring memories of friends, dances, crushes. She loved seeing the faceless mannequins styled up and standing above her with attitude. It was as if the entire section of Junior Miss promised happiness, perfection— that she too could one day accessorize perfectly and stand tall, her hip jutting out and her pointer finger elegantly positioned alongside her jaw, her mouth slightly, suggestively open in an expression of superiority.

Over the years, she learned that most young girls had also been obsessed with the store as a path to their better selves, which was achievable only through the adornment of patterned polyester blends and gold-plated jewelry. Like Taylor, many of them had grown up blindly pursuing that dream, eventually finding themselves with thousands of dollars of department store credit card debt. Looking at her own statement one day, reality struck, and she knew that sooner or later she was going to have to face the consequence of her consumer pursuits. Her debt had ballooned to over twenty thousand dollars. OVERDUE was stamped in bold, red letters across the top of the statement, the same red as the new lipstick she had just acquired. Taylor's thoughts turned to how great she would feel going out that night with her ruby lips, and she promptly dropped the bill in the trash.

In her Arizona suburb, consumerism was as popular a pastime as golf or tummy tucks. Just months before her own comeuppance, collection agencies had chased down hundreds of debtors just like her. When they were unable to pay, they went straight to jail. But soon the jails became overcrowded and wanted to expand, and the taxpayers complained that they shouldn't be held responsible for what the department stores had instigated.

Local lawmakers, who once looked down on "east coast liberals" as un-American, now pointed to New York in solidarity and cited that voters had justly held fast food restaurants accountable for health care costs. Armed with the New York precedent and highlighting the billions spent on marketing, the government made the case that the department stores enabled and encouraged the people of their town to accumulate designer denim and handbag debt. Thus, they argued, the department stores should be part of the solution.

The department stores, threatened by diminished bottom lines and worried about the negative press, decided to negotiate with voters. Together with the courts, they created a program that would allow the debtors to pay off what they owed by working as employees and living in the store. A section of the floor above the showroom, where the big wigs had offices and the security staff sat watching, was converted to dormitory-like quarters where the offenders slept at night, while during the day they were employed as retail clerks and maintenance workers.

As each person got close to working off their owed amount, they would return to the judge who would determine whether they needed to stay in the program or be released from it.

Taylor had spent fifteen months living and working here. The last time she was up for release, Taylor hesitated just a tad too long when the judge asked whether she'd learned her lesson. He ordered four more months but directed her to transition into a new program that would allow her to live at home while working at the store, making room for new debtors.

Now she'd finally served her time and here she was, her last day of service and facing a complete return to normal life in just eight hours. She shut the car door and began walking toward the unadorned "Employees Only" entrance. As she pulled the heavy door open, the hot metal knob burned her hand, and the air conditioning blew cold on her face.

During her final months, Taylor finally accepted her truth: she *needed* to accumulate. The financial transaction was really the only part that had caused her trouble. Gathering new things made her a better person, and wasn't self-improvement a worthwhile goal?

She solved the problem by simply removing the financial part of the process. She started by pocketing a few small items here and there: a Swatch watch, some dangly earrings, a scarf. By her final week she'd set the bar high: a pair of gold Jessica Simpson heels that had just come in. She knew those would make her very happy. Of course, she experienced moments of honesty about what was happening, but each time she was quick to attribute her behavior to self-care. She had been depressed, but with thoughtful reflection and resourcefulness, she'd learned how to move herself out of that depression all on her own.

The store was busy today, and Taylor hardly had time to scope out any new inventory for her collection at home. She half-expected a celebration on her last day, but ever since she'd entered the transition program and begun her habit of stealing, she had pulled away from her friends at the store. It had become essential that she not be close to anyone lest they feel entitled to dig around in her bags without permission.

As she moved through her day, she felt a force of power rising up in her chest. She was right about those Jessica Simpson heels: they *would* make her feel great. But as she tried to rejoice in her forthcoming freedom and envision herself in those pumps, she felt dread about her future. She'd no longer have an excuse to spend every day at the store, and she didn't know other department stores like she knew this one. How would she continue to have all that she wanted? How bored would she be without the excitement of acquiring new things? She wrapped up her shift, and as a farewell gift to herself, grabbed a small bottle of Chanel No. 5 and slid it up her sleeve with the deftness of a magician. *Sad one minute, happy the next*, she thought with pride. *I'm in complete control.*

Pulling up to her mother's house, Taylor noticed a few cars in the driveway. *A celebration after all*, she thought and smiled to herself, wishing she were wearing those heels. She flung open the door, expecting a grand "Congratulations!" Instead, she laid eyes on a silent and tense crew made up of her mother, sisters, and case worker.

There on the breakfast table sat a pile of all her stolen things. Taylor stopped in her tracks, feeling her face flush and her heart drop into her stomach, imagining her mother discovering the stash under her bed, in her closet, in her drawers. She tried to think quickly. Could she explain her way out of this? Taylor's caseworker stared at her with a blank expression, while her mother was suddenly all smiles. It was disconcerting, confusing.

"There you are, T! Come on in here, sweetheart!" Her mother slipped her arm around her waist. "Honey, we wanted to celebrate your last day! You've come so far!"

Her caseworker, Ryder, looked doubtful; standing against the counter with his arms crossed.

"Isn't it nice that Ryder came by?" They both looked his way.

"I didn't know you were having a family party, just stopped by to congratulate you. What is all this?" He gestured to the pile.

Taylor looked to her mom, whose eyes betrayed a conspiratorial glimmer.

"Gifts for her!" her mother said emphatically. "She's been through so much." Her mother winked at her. "So proud of you, honey."

Taylor was momentarily stunned. She knew it was time to say, *Thanks Mom, but don't take this on for me. I am responsible for this—I stole these things and I will pay the price.* She could see herself doing the right thing; she even anticipated the relief that might follow. But those words did not come.

"Mom, you're the best. But I don't need all this. My happiness comes from a truer place now."

"Taylor, honey, that is wonderful, but I've already taken off all the tags and thrown away the receipts. I guess you'll have to keep it all! Now, let's get this party started! Who wants a drink?"

Ryder shook his head and turned to leave. "I'll show myself out."

Taylor called after him then jutted out her hip and brought her finger to her jaw. With her eye slightly twitching, she asked, "Can't you stay to celebrate with us? Mom, do we have any cheese? Let's use this beautiful new cheese board you got me! And somebody please hand me those fabulous heels!"

Co-Existence

Whenever she felt on the verge of defeat, Beatrix inserted the old memory chip that had been passed down from her great-grandmother. The information absorbed into her psyche from the slot near her temple; data relayed from her optic nerve right into her frontal lobe. It was like reading, but more visceral, personal. It was a reminder and a fortifying boost: there was more to live for, if she could just keep fighting.

Her grandfather himself had lived to be 138 years old, so the chip that had belonged to *his* mother was ancient now, as were the memories it contained. As a young girl, Beatrix had been curious about how society had functioned before her time. Her parents had told her things that other parents didn't bother telling, like how children used to learn in schools, studying art, history, literature, science, even reading made-up stories.

There was no time for excesses like that anymore. Youth were taught only what was needed for survival. "Naturals"—humans who were still unchanged referred to themselves in this way in order to differentiate from their counterparts—shed all knowledge more than a few months old unless it was critical. It took dedicated effort to retain anything else, but unlike the rest of her kind, Beatrix worked at it regularly. It felt crucial to her for reasons she was unable to express.

One evening several years ago her parents never came home, and she realized that she was on her own. She retrieved the box her great-grandmother left to her, which she buried under the floor in every bunker she'd ever stayed in, then found a "doctor" who performed the specialized surgery. Now, when she had a moment of safe time, she injected her heirloom into its slot and soaked the stories in.

One of the last times Beatrix saw her parents, they'd tried to convey to her the notion of true attachment that they, like her grandparents before, claimed to share. They called it love. As she understood it, it was a tangling of emotions, a shared vision of the future and past. She had committed the idea of love to memory after absorbing it several times, but it was a concept she was ill-equipped to truly grasp. She found that her friends didn't care to hear about love or anything else she'd discovered about the past. In fact, they dismissed all of their ancestors' possessions as useless. She didn't personally know anyone who'd had the slot surgery. Evolution had trained Naturals to operate in the here and now, nothing more.

Stories from the chip told her how generations ago, Zombies had held only a fictional role in society. But once they gained a foothold in reality, life for Naturals changed fast. Beatrix learned that many minorities had spent centuries fighting or breeding their way to majority status and the societal benefits that came with it. Zombies had perfected this quest because they couldn't help but succeed; their instinct to devour their way through the existing population had the beneficial result of not only removing Naturals from the world, but simultaneously adding more Zombies. Biology was what made Zombies dominant, and it turned out to be a much stronger force to overcome than ideology.

Once Naturals realized that Zombies completely owned the power of numbers, most of them gave up. Many took their own lives rather than let themselves be forced into joining the Zombies' ranks against their wills and endangering their own kin.

Over the years, mutual ground rules had developed and were tacitly agreed upon. Zombies had developed their own daytime culture and no longer were solely interested in hunting, choosing instead to only attack at night. Once Naturals realized they might survive this nightmare, they stopped hiding out all day in their bunkers, which were not much more than small shelters dug into a hillside or makeshift sheds, each with a disguised but strongly fortified entry. They were outfitted with only a couple of blankets to make sleep comfortable and the few possessions deemed worthy enough to take with them when they relocated every few months. After a bunker was left uninhabited for a long period of time, it might be used again by someone else. Zombies were efficient killers but not very strategic or collaborative hunters, so it was fairly easy to fool them.

Naturals wanted to live again, even if it was in these constrained circumstances. Yoga, baseball, and other nostalgic pastimes were revived. As long as the sun was up, both groups were able to cross paths without incident. Eventually, the population ratio held steady as if nature had found a good balance. Procreation was now solely driven by the need to sustain the Natural population and maintain that balance. In each region there was a small circle of people around the same age who mixed and matched in rotation as they tried to expand the gene pool. Still a teenager, Beatrix had only been involved in the process for a little over a year and had not yet become pregnant, but she knew that would soon change.

Beatrix had a few good friends, but once she came of age, she met Rowan. After one rotation in which they had been assigned to each other, she felt a need to remain in his presence. They began spending a lot of time together in their bunkers.

As weeks passed, Beatrix and Rowan moved beyond practical strategizing to discussing their futures, sharing hopes and what-ifs. He was different than any other friend she'd had. He carried his own small collection of books. She had never met anyone besides her parents who even owned books, and the simple act of touching them and holding them took her back to a happier time, when she was young and still had her parents to protect her from the world that she now had to face alone. He read to her each night as they huddled in darkness.

He called her "B," and she loved the familiarity, the casualness, the intimacy it evoked. His family had not kept a chip, and he was fascinated by hers and wanted to learn all it contained. She told him about her great-grandparents, and they discussed the concepts of connection, of desire, of love. With him, she finally began to understand.

One day, after a particularly disorienting and exhilarating physical interlude, Beatrix and Rowan were feeling unusually relaxed and let their guard down. He stepped out of the bunker to enjoy the last bit of light and evening air, but the earth had already spun them too close to darkness.

When she heard his screams, the pain crushed her as she collapsed to the floor, useless, locked in on the safe side of the door. In the hours that followed, she told herself that perhaps he'd escaped before the damage was complete. But when he didn't return the next day or the day after that, she sunk into a state of despair. It took over a year just to train herself to block the memory of that night whenever it reappeared. But she could never fully stop herself from wondering if he, even in his new condition, remembered her.

Beatrix grew accustomed to passing her time differently, and mostly alone. She forced herself to go to a weekly yoga class, even though there were only one or two other Naturals that practiced in a room full of Zombies. These odds were fairly common at restaurants, theaters, and libraries, and she was used to it. She knew it would have been unbelievable to her ancestors that she was doing sun salutations in harmony with someone who could be ripping her insides out as soon as the sun set. They even exchanged head nods as greetings; as antagonistic ethnic groups in the past might have done, feigning tolerance for one another just to maintain civility.

One day, just after laying out her yoga mat and sitting down in lotus, there he was: walking right past her to a spot at the opposite end of the room. She squeezed her eyes shut then allowed herself to look at him again. It was Rowan, there was no doubt, and she searched for evidence of his change. She knew he must have been converted or else he would have come back to her. She knew what she'd heard that night. He had definite physical identifiers, like the repugnant wounds on his shoulders and back. And yet there was something about him that was unaltered: he had the same softness in those piercing green eyes.

Using all her training, she refocused herself hundreds of times and somehow made it through the class. It was getting dark earlier now, and she needed to get back to her bunker within the hour. But instead, she hung around outside the studio, re-lacing her shoes, stalling to see where he would go. He walked out, not lumbering as much as the others did, but she saw that his gait had changed. He turned with a slow but purposeful stride up the block toward the shopping district. She gave him a good head start and then followed.

Her heart jumped when he turned into a store they used to visit together which sold sundries, tools, and most importantly, books. Beatrix felt a surge of hope that the human was still somewhere inside him. She watched him from a safe distance as he started perusing a small bookshelf. She squinted and tried to read the titles he seemed most interested in. Suddenly, he looked back at her before she could look away.

"Hi, Beatrix."

She scolded herself for her carelessness, stunned by the direct contact.

"Oh, hi…" *Get away from him…* "I was just…" *Run! Now!* "I've seen you around. I was hoping we'd talk sometime. I miss you. Us."

He smiled at her as he spoke but was working hard to keep his lips closed. She focused on his eyes, which drew her in as they always had.

He leaned in toward her. "It's getting late. You shouldn't be out much longer." His closeness sent a chill through her body, and goose bumps rose on her forearms. He looked down and saw them. She shook her head as if to clear the fog that was building.

"Yes, you're right. I should be going." She reached down for the yoga mat she had dropped and at the same time noticed through the window that the sun had sunk low, filling the sky with swipes of pink and orange. In the street she saw only Zombies; the Naturals had all gone indoors. She was angry with herself for slipping like this, yet her feet were glued to the floor.

"Beatrix?" His voice penetrated her thoughts, and she locked eyes with him. Those emerald eyes. "Let me walk you home." His sincere voice broke her, and all her feelings rushed back, scattering her determination like dust.

"I don't know. I'll be okay." She could take care of herself. She always had. She didn't need an escort, especially not a Zombie, but she had no words.

He pressed her. "You could tell me the rest of that story about your great-grandmother. I will never forget that night, Beatrix. Do you remember it? I've always wondered if we'd be able to recreate it. I mean, before…you know. It was like a book."

Yes, of course she remembered. That night they realized their connection was something more than a population goal, more than a friendship with someone the same age. It was real and it was theirs, and it changed everything about their outlook for their future—until it was all ripped away in an instant.

"Let's go," he said decisively. He grabbed her mat and her arm, and she felt herself giving in. The Zombies were out in droves now. "Don't look at any of them, B. Don't make eye contact."

The sun was barely a sliver now and was so low she could see it moving.

They walked quickly, and she realized he was going directly to her bunker, even though she'd told him nothing about where she lived.

"It's this one, right?"

The entrance was hidden, but she could see now that it was not disguised well enough. "How did you know where I was staying?" She had been in one place too long.

He reached out to touch her neck. "I've been watching you. I wanted to make sure none of them got to you, B. I've thought about this moment so many times."

She felt herself crumble. This feeling—it was no longer a

part of her life. But as they stood there, his deteriorated skin touching hers, she realized that because of him she needed it, it wasn't optional or negotiable, and that need would never leave her. She was so tired of living with muscles tensed, constantly scanning her surroundings with nervous eyes, plotting routes. She stuck out her wrist that contained an embedded passkey and held it up in front of a small red light. The heavy entrance clicked open.

They stepped across the threshold together. She knew she should push him out and lock the door, but she couldn't. She wanted him there. She felt his hand on the small of her back, then his other hand firmly but gently gripping her wrist and guiding it once again in front of the sensor from the inside, barricading them in her safe zone. His squeeze intensified, and a shallow breath stuck high in her chest as she felt his mouth coming in to kiss her. She gagged as she smelled the putrid stench that escaped his lips, but there wasn't time to adjust before he tore at the flesh of her neck.

Acknowledgments

For decades, we've found in one another that rarest type of friend—the one who actually wants to hear what the other dreamt the night before. In all of their bewildering, mismatched, nonsensical detail, we have spent years writing about our dreams and sharing them back and forth, responding to each other with analysis and insight.

Many years passed before we realized we had amassed a large number of these exchanges. Most of the dream descriptions were ridiculous, but now and then, they took the form of narratives that made us laugh, or think, or wonder. These are the dreams that we began to explore as inspiration for creating short fiction. Many edits and revisions later, we present this collection of stories.

We are grateful to our friends and family for reading through many iterations and giving us honest feedback. We also thank our husbands for supporting the time we needed away from our families and other obligations over the past year.

This project—and our enjoyment of its process—took a pivotal turn when our dear friend Amy Peltonen, a gifted reader and thoughtful critic, contributed her perspective and opened our eyes to new possibilities. More importantly, we have the added fortune of rekindling our friendship with her. For that, we will forever be grateful.

Artwork and Photography courtesy of:

Amy Perl, cover photo: *Welcome to the Circus*

Ginger and Gus Collins, Part 1 photo: *What you see, Mama?*

Ginger Collins, Part 2 photo: *Heads or Tails*

Hugo Q Jonathan Bours, Part 3 illustration: *Peaceful Night*

Ginger Collins and Pamela Griner, authors' page photo: *Shadow Toast in Ensenada*

Book cover designed by George Bours

About the Authors

Pamela is an independent film producer with an affinity for hip-hop, snowboarding, coffee, and tacos. She occasionally spends evenings outside of live music venues trying to score tickets to see her favorite bands. She lives in Los Angeles with her husband, her burgeoning writer of a son, and her twin daughters. She's been eating batteries in her dreams since pregnancy. This is her first book.

Ginger is an organizational change management consultant, which is code for "warm and fuzzy stabilizing force amidst corporate chaos." She once rode a bike from San Francisco to Los Angeles, but now prefers a long hike in the Rockies. Ginger loves conversing with strangers in foreign countries, even without a small friend in her backpack. She lives in Denver with her husband and son. This is also her first book.